THE LAND OF GIANTS

AN EROTIC FAIRYTALE

VICTORIA RUSH

VOLUME 2

CLOVER'S FANTASY ADVENTURES -
BOOK 2

COPYRIGHT

For the uninhibited...

WANT TO AMP UP YOUR SEX LIFE?

Sign up for my newsletter to receive more free books and other steamy stuff. Discover a hundred different ways to wet your whistle!

Victoria Rush Erotica

1

Jessop stared up at the two-hundred-foot-tall gate to the castle of Gargaton and shook his head.

"Are you sure this is a good idea?" he said to his traveling companions. "We're barely the size of *gnats* compared to these people. Even Rex looks no larger than a horsefly in comparison. I'm not sure how much help he'll be if we get into any trouble in there."

"That could work to our advantage," Clover said. "Being this small means we'll be harder to see. And we'll be able to hide in little crevices where they can't reach us."

"But I thought you said you wanted to make *contact*? To see if the king can help you find your missing waterfall?"

"Not until we scope things out a little first. Let's see what we're up against before we venture inside. Rex can give us a birds-eye view of the place and help us find the location of the king and queen, then we can decide how to proceed."

"Do you think he'll wait for us if we decide to go inside?" Tara said. "How do we know he won't fly off and abandon us at the first opportunity?"

"He seems to have grown quite fond of us since we

healed his wing," Clover said, rubbing the dragon's scaly neck. "Besides, he knows as long as he stays with us that he can count on a regular lunch of roast boar. Right, boy? You wouldn't leave us in the lurch, would you?"

Rex swiped his face against the side of Clover's body, then the trio climbed aboard his back and she pulled gently back on his ears, signaling for him to take flight. As they soared over the palace ramparts, their eyes widened at the enormous scale of the fortress. With towers rising almost a thousand feet off the ground, the highest reaches were obscured by clouds. The whole place looked like something out of a distant world, built to ten times the scale of any other structure in Abbynthia.

"How will we know where to find the king and queen?" Jessop said, squinting through the heavy mist. "This place is enormous!"

"It stands to reason they'd be near the top, right?" Clover said, pointing to an elevated terrace illuminated by a shaft of sunlight. "Let's check out that platform over there. At least there's a place to land."

Clover pulled on Rex's left ear, shifting her weight forward, and the dragon angled downward, landing gently on the marble-tiled balcony. Two large French doors lay open, leading to a huge anteroom dominated by a giant four-poster bed. Gilded curtains surrounding the bed fluttered in the breeze floating in from the terrace, and Clover noticed the pale skin of somebody's body shifting restlessly in the bed. As the three friends crept closer, they gasped when a naked girl suddenly sat up, stretching her arms above her head. Rex flapped his wings excitedly, and the girl turned her head to peer outside.

"Who goes there?" she said. "Is it you nettlesome mice again?"

She got out of bed and picked up a broom sitting in a corner of the room, then crept toward the open doors of the terrace, holding the broom like a weapon, preparing to swat the unwanted intruders away. Clover pressed her hand against Rex's chest and inched backwards with the others behind a large clay pot, motioning for the dragon to stay quiet. The girl prowled around the terrace searching for the mice, and when she peered behind the pot noticing the group, she gasped.

"Little people!" she cried, lurching away. "How did you get up here?"

The three friends peered at one another with their mouths agape, unsure how to respond. The girl barely looked out of her teens, but with the full voluptuous figure of a grown woman. Her giant breasts jiggled as she moved her massive figure, and the bush between her legs glistened with a fresh dew as if she'd been touching herself before her unexpected interruption. She had long, wavy blonde hair with bright blue eyes and full, rosebud lips. Clover had never seen such a beautiful woman her entire life, and she could feel her own pussy moistening as she peered up at the girl.

"Um, we flew up on our dragon and–" she said.

"A *dragon*!" the girl exclaimed, leaning over to inspect the group more closely. "I've never seen one of those before. He's so cute! May I touch him?"

Rex hissed as the girl reached her hand down toward them, then she quickly retracted it.

"You better not," Clover said. "He can be a bit testy until he gets to know people better. And you definitely look a bit intimidating..."

"I don't mean to hurt you," the girl said. "It's just that I've never met little people before. What brings you so far away from home?"

"My friend is a little lost," Tara said, stepping out slowly from behind the pot. "She fell through some kind of portal and can't find her way back. We thought maybe you could help us."

"I don't know about that," the girl said. "But if anyone would know where to find such a portal, it would be my father, the king. He knows everything about this land. Would you like to come inside and meet him?"

Tara looked at her friends and they shrugged. It was obvious they were smitten by the larger-than-life princess as they ran their eyes over her creamy, naked body.

"Okay," she said. "But are you sure it's safe? Will the king receive us?"

"He will if I introduce you."

"Do you mind if we leave the dragon outside? He gets a bit claustrophobic in closed spaces."

"Of course," the girl said, leading the group into her bedroom and closing the terrace doors softly behind her.

Then she knelt down on one knee, cupping her hands over the floor.

"Why don't you make yourself comfortable on my settee while we get to know one another a little better? I'm dying to know all about your way of life in the little people world."

The three friends looked at one another for a moment, then stepped gingerly into the girl's hands as she lifted them onto the upholstered footstool at the end of her bed. Not even bothering to put on any clothes, she sat cross-legged at the end of the bed, peering at them curiously.

"My name's Ophelia. What are yours?"

"I'm Clover," Clover said. "These are my friends Tara and Jessop. And our dragon is named Rex."

"You've taken him as a *pet*?"

"I'm not sure pet is the proper term for him," Tara said. "But he does seem to have taken an affinity toward us, and he comes in handy when we need to cover a lot of ground in a hurry."

"So I see," Ophelia said, glancing outside the doors at Rex peering back at them with a forlorn expression. "Where are you all from?"

"I'm from a place far away called Tennessee," Clover said. "And Tara's from the land of Abbynthia."

"What about *this* handsome fellow?" Ophelia said, poking Jessop playfully in his stomach.

"He's from the Norseland," Clover said, noticing Jessop still staring up at the gorgeous naked princess with his mouth agape. "His father is lord of the Kingdom of Stordalen."

"A *lord*?" the girl said, raising an eyebrow. "That should help when it comes time to introducing you to my father. How did you all manage to come together from such far-flung lands?"

"That's a long story," Clover said. "The short version is that we bumped into one another."

"And the dragon?"

Clover turned her head toward Rex as she listened to him pining outside the window.

"We found him injured in the forest and nursed him back to health. Now he seems stuck to us like glue."

"I can see why," Ophelia said, darting her eyes over Clover and Tara's plump bosoms. "Are the three of you just friends, or something *more*?"

"Um...well," Clover hesitated. "We've become very good friends in the short time we've been together."

"If you don't mind my asking," the princess said. "How do you little people propagate?"

"I suppose in the same way Gargatons do," she said, peering into the dark shadow below the princess's crossed legs.

"I've never actually engaged in any contact with another of my kind," the princess said. "I've just learned from the scriptures my parents allow me to read. From what I can tell, the men and women have different parts designed to join together and that it's supposed to be quite pleasurable."

"It is indeed," Tara said. "But it's not just the men and women who join together. It can be just as pleasurable for the women and the men to engage in sexual contact with each of their kind as well."

"Really?" Ophelia said, inching closer to the three little ones on the end of her bed. "I've never heard of that kind of thing. Can you show me how it's done? I feel so ill-prepared in these matters."

Clover and Tara paused as they peered at one another for a moment, then they smiled.

"I suppose we could give it a try," Tara said. "But are you sure the king won't mind? It sounds as if he's keeping you sheltered for a reason..."

"What he doesn't know won't hurt him," Ophelia said. "I've been locked up in this tower for so long, I need a little distraction. It gets pretty lonely being left to my own devices all the time."

"Anything to help with the education of such a pretty princess," Tara smiled, beginning to strip off her clothes.

Clover did the same and when they were completely naked, they sat facing one another, shifting their hips closer together until their vulvas touched. As they began to rock their hips together, they leaned forward, moaning into each other's mouths.

"Does that feel as good as when a *man* touches you there?" Ophelia asked, beginning to spread her legs apart on the bed.

"Yes, in a different kind of way," Tara nodded, pinching Clover's hardening nipples between her fingers. "Have you ever touched yourself down there? It feels good no matter how you're touched if you're sufficiently aroused."

"Sometimes," Ophelia said, drifting her fingers between her legs to caress her glistening pussy. "But it sure feels a lot better when I'm this excited."

As the two friends rubbed their pussies together, they turned their heads to watch the princess towering over them while she fingered her dripping vulva. Looking like a giant clam mere inches away from their faces, the movement of the princess's hand on her slit sent a gentle breeze wafting over their bodies while the slurping sound of her wet pussy sounded like a roaring waterfall.

"You're incredibly beautiful," Tara said, feeling their juices spreading over the inside of her and Clover's thighs as the two girls became more excited watching the pretty princess play with herself. "It's a shame you've never been permitted to share your body with anyone else. It's even better when you can feel the touch of someone else."

"I wish you girls were closer to my size," Ophelia groaned. "I'd love to feel your beautiful bodies rubbing up against mine the way you're doing now. It's making me feel some strange new sensations."

Clover noticed Ophelia's fingers moving more rapidly over the apple-sized nub at the top of her folds as a redness began to spread over her cheeks and chest.

"Have you never climaxed before?" she said, feeling her own pleasure rapidly rising within her.

"What's *that*?" Ophelia said.

"I have a feeling you're about to find out," Clover said. "Just keep doing what you're doing and relax as you let the pleasure wash over you. I'm going to come with you. I've never seen anything this sexy in all my life..."

"Oh!" Ophelia suddenly grunted. "Something's happening. It feels so strange..."

"Just let it go, baby," Tara said, moaning louder as she flapped her dripping pussy harder against Clover's burning cunt. "It's a beautiful thing when a woman climaxes."

"*Oh God, oh God...*" Ophelia huffed, beginning to go into convulsions. "It feels so good! *Uhnnnn!*"

As she began to tremble, the weight of her giant body shook the entire bed and the attached footstool, sending the two girls bouncing up in the air while they clung onto one another in the throes of their own powerful orgasm. Somehow the trampoline effect of the shaking settee added to their excitement, and they moaned loudly along with the princess while they took in erotic show before them.

When the three women finally stopped panting from their simultaneous orgasms, they heard a different kind of moaning coming from behind them. When they peered over to the other side of the settee, they saw Jessop staring at them sheepishly while he jackhammered his hard-as-a-rock erection.

2

"So *that's* what an orgasm feels like!" Ophelia panted, still coming down from her powerful climax.

"Pretty good, huh?" Clover said. "And it feels even better when you do it with someone else."

"I *wish*," Ophelia said. "But my father is a bit over-protective and seems hell-bent on choosing a high-born suitor for me. And he expects me to remain chaste until marriage."

"What about *Jessop*?" Tara said, only half-kidding. "His father is a lord."

"If you can find a way to grow him ten times as large," Ophelia said, peering at Jessop's still twitching cock, "he'd suit me just fine. But I'm not exactly sure he'd be able to squire me a full-size heir in his current state."

"That's too bad," Clover said, noticing her friend staring up at the beautiful princess with wide eyes. "Because he seems quite smitten with you."

"Do men and women do it the same way as you girls?" the princess asked. "Is it just a matter of rubbing your body parts together until everybody has an orgasm?"

"That's the essence of it," Clover chuckled. "Although

technically, the woman doesn't need to orgasm in order to procreate. When the man climaxes, he injects his seed into his partner."

"Even if it's another *man*?"

"I guess that depends on how they're interacting exactly," Clover said. "There's an almost infinite number of ways to stimulate your partner to orgasm."

"Can you show me how a man and a woman do it? It would be nice to have some idea of what to expect on my wedding night."

"I suppose so," Clover said, peering at Jessop's turgid tool. "But maybe there's a way for you to simulate the experience while we demonstrate how it's done. Do you have something a little bigger you can put inside you while you watch this time?"

Ophelia's eyes widened as her pussy suddenly twitched.

"You mean shaped like a *cock*?"

"Exactly."

The princess peered around her room, resting her gaze on a bowl of fruit sitting on a sideboard, then she walked over and picked up a long purple gourd shaped like an oversize inkberry.

"How about *this*? It's about the right size and shape. It even looks like the color of Jessop's penis."

"That should work," Clover smiled. "I have experience using something like that myself. I think you'll find it's a useful substitute for the real thing when you're feeling needy."

Ophelia resumed her position on the foot of the bed facing the three friends, then she spread her legs apart with the tip of the gourd at the opening to her dripping slit.

"How do I do this exactly?"

"You can watch us to get an idea," Clover said, pressing

Jessop's back down onto the settee as she straddled his cock facing the princess. "Turn the gourd around so that it curves upward. I think you'll find that stimulates you in a more pleasing manner."

As Clover lowered herself onto Jessop's pole, Ophelia slowly inserted the tuber into her pussy, moaning as it slid over her sensitive G-spot ,with the thick end pressed up against her clit.

"Oh God," she groaned. "This feels *so* much better than my hand."

"There's something to be said for *penetration* at the right time," Clover panted as she rocked her hips over Jessop's tight balls.

"Is that how you normally do it?" Ophelia said, thrusting the purple vegetable in and out of her snatch as she watched Clover and Jessop fucking directly in front of her. "In that position?"

"Not always," Clover said, lifting herself off Jessop's dick to position herself facing his head this time. "It's nice to mix it up from time to time to create a little variety. It can get a bit boring if you do it the same way every time."

"Speaking of..." Ophelia said, noticing Tara sitting off to the side circling her clit while she watched the princess diddling herself. "What about your *other* friend? She looks a little left out of the fun."

"There's lots of ways we can stimulate each other," Clover said, motioning for Tara to join her and Jessop. "That's the beauty of having all these body parts to work with. There's never any shortage of ways to stimulate one another."

Tara kneeled over Jessop's head and lowered her pussy onto his face while she leaned forward to kiss Clover. As the three lovers began groaning in pleasure, Ophelia pounded the gourd harder against her dripping hole. Droplets of lubrication began spurting out of her pussy in the direction of the threesome, who moaned even louder from the sensation of the erotic shower.

"This feels different than when I touch myself with my *hand*," Ophelia panted, pulling her knees together. "It almost feels like I have to pee."

"That's because you're stimulating a very special spot inside your pussy," Clover said. "Sometimes, if you massage it just right, you can actually make yourself ejaculate like a man. But don't worry, it's not actually pee. Just let it go when you feel yourself getting close to climax. It feels even *better* when you orgasm that way."

"Oh my God," Ophelia grunted. "It feels like I'm going to *explode*! Are you sure this is safe?"

"As long as you don't mind soaking your sheets a little bit," Clover chuckled, rubbing her tits against Tara as Jessop began thrusting his hips harder against her ass. "And having the most incredible climax you've ever experienced in your life."

"If this is what having sex with a *man* is like, I hope my father marries me off soon," Ophelia grunted, feeling her pleasure approaching the tipping point. "Because I could do this all day, every day!"

Suddenly she growled like a wild animal and arched her back as she thrust the gourd as deep into her pussy as she could. While giant jets of fluid began spurting out of her hole in the direction of the trio on the settee, she began flapping her thighs in an out in delirious ecstasy, wailing at the top of her lungs. When the others felt the waterfall of juices drenching their naked bodies, they began to quiver and groan in simultaneous pleasure. For many long seconds, the four of them shuddered in delight while the bedsprings noisily creaked and the room filled with a cacophony of sensual noise.

Suddenly, the door to Ophelia's parlor burst open and a huge man wearing long robes stood in the opening.

"What the hell is going on in here?" he bellowed. "Are you alright, Ophelia?"

The princess looked at him in horror as she clamped her legs shut, pulling the bedspread over her bare shoulders.

The man looked at her dumbfounded for a moment, then when he saw the three little people sitting atop one another naked, he rushed forward, encircling them with his hands.

"What are these creatures doing in here?" he said, peering at Ophelia's dripping thighs. "Have you been–?"

"I'm sorry father!" Ophelia said, curling up with the bedspread wrapped around her. "These little people flew up on my terrace and I was just talking with them..."

"It doesn't look like you were just *talking*," he said, swiping his hand over her soaking sheets. "What kind of perversion is this that you'd want to have *sex* with little people?"

"We weren't actually having sex–"

"*Somebody* sure as hell was," the king said, opening his palms to peer at the trio still balled up in his oversize hands. "And how did they fly up here?"

The king suddenly turned when he heard a strange squawking sound coming from outside the terrace doors where Rex was flapping his wings angrily against the glass, desperate to save his friends from the clutches of the giant ogre.

"A miniature *dragon*?" the king said. "What other surprises have you brought into our castle?"

"Please don't hurt them, father! They're my friends. They were just trying to help me."

"*Help* you? By putting on a carnal display of debauchery in front of my chaste daughter? We'll see what the queen has to say about this."

He peered around the room looking for a place to contain the little people, then he walked over to the glass fruit bowl and emptied it of its contents before dropping them inside and placing a large book over the top to trap them inside. Then he flung open the terrace doors, trying to capture the dragon. But Rex quickly took flight, spraying a jet of fire in his direction as he ducked and swatted at the creature unsuccessfully. After a few minutes of trying to swat him down with the broom, he stormed back into the princess's room, slamming the terrace doors behind him.

"Are there any *more* of those where he came from?" the king said, lifting the book off the fruit bowl to glare at the shivering trio. "Does he have a full-size mother I should be worried about?"

"No," Clover said. "We found him in the land of the little people."

"What are you doing here then?"

"We thought maybe you could help us," Clover said, trying to cover up her naked body with her crossed arms. "I got lost and can't find my way back home."

"Where exactly are you from?"

"The United States. A little town called Asheville, Tennessee."

"Never heard of the place," the king said. "It's not on any map I've ever seen."

"If you let us go," Tara said, stepping forward. "We'll be on our way and not bother you or your daughter any further. We mean you no harm."

"*Harm?*" the king snorted. "You little people are hardly in any position to threaten my kingdom."

He swiped his thick finger against Tara's naked body with a sneer.

"Though I might be able to find some *other* way you can amuse me with your special talents."

He placed the book back atop the bowl and curled it under his arm, striding back toward the parlor's entrance door.

"Where are you taking them?" Ophelia cried, chasing after him with her bedspread dragging across the floor.

"This is no concern of yours any longer," the king said, turning around to place his arm in front of Ophelia's chest. "They will be dealt with in the appropriate manner. You and I will be having words a little later. For now, I want you to get yourself cleaned up and put on some proper clothes. There'll be no more erotic escapades with your little friends or anyone else for that matter for a very long time."

As the king slammed the door behind him, Ophelia peered out onto her terrace where Rex sat perched on a railing looking back at her with sad eyes, whining like an abandoned puppy.

3

The three friends peered at one another with frightened eyes as their bodies jostled inside the glass bowl while the king clomped down a long corridor.

"I told you this was a bad idea," Jessop said to Clover, holding his hand against the side of the bowl to keep himself from falling over.

"We made this decision together," she said, bumping up against Tara as it tipped and turned under the king's arm.

"Yes, to investigate if the king could help us find your way home. Not to put on a lewd display for his virgin daughter!"

"I didn't hear you complaining while you were staring up at her giant tits."

"Stop it, you two!" Tara interjected. "This isn't helping. We should be thinking about how we're going to get ourselves out of this unfortunate situation."

"Have you got any bright ideas?" Jessop said, rapping his knuckles against the hard surface of the glass. "Because in case you haven't noticed, this thing only has one exit, and I'm pretty sure we won't be able to budge that giant book trapping us in here."

"We'll just have to talk reasonably with the king," Tara said. "He doesn't have any reason to harm us, and if he doesn't let us go right away, we'll simply bide our time until we find the right moment to escape."

"It sounds like he's pretty pissed," Jessop said. "I didn't exactly like the sound of his comment that we'll be dealt with in the appropriate manner."

As the king approached the end of the hall, he swung open a door leading into an even larger bedroom than Ophelia's. A middle-aged woman sat up looking alarmed in the middle of the bed, peering at the bowl under the king's arm.

"What in heaven's name is going on?" she said. "Did you find out what all that commotion was about?"

"I did," the king said, holding up the bowl for the woman to inspect its contents. "And you're not going to believe what I saw. Three little people fornicating with our daughter!"

The woman squinted her eyes, peering at the three friends cowering inside the bowl.

"They're *naked!*"

"Exactly," the king said. "And so was Ophelia. Apparently, they were engaged in some kind of kinky orgy."

"But these people are far too *little* to have sex with our daughter. What exactly were they doing?"

"They were rubbing their bodies together while Ophelia was looking on touching herself."

The queen leaned in closer to inspect the naked figures of the trio, then tapped her fingers on the outside surface like she was peering into a fish bowl.

"I can see why," she smiled. "They're quite comely, for little people. They must have been putting on quite a stimulating show."

"What do you propose I do with them?" the king said. "Throw them over the balcony, or should I just flush them down the toilet?"

"There's no need to take such drastic measures," the queen said. "If they're so interested in putting on an erotic show for their hosts, perhaps we can find a way for them to amuse *us* for a while."

"With *little people*?" the king rattled. "They're no better than *vermin*!"

"Oh come now, dear," the queen smiled, stroking her husband's arm softly. "I know you have a certain affinity for young girls, the smaller the better. And from the looks of it, these creatures barely look past the age of puberty. I kind of like the looks of the boy, even if he does have a tiny little pecker."

"What exactly did you have in mind?" the king said.

"Why don't you put the bowl down on the night table while we watch them carry on their little show. You're always looking for new ways to spice up our sex life. This is definitely something a little different."

The queen patted the bed beside her as she began to pull off her negligee.

"Take off your clothes and come join me while we have a little fun. We haven't had this many naked people in our bed chamber since after our wedding night."

The king paused for a moment as he looked at his wife, then he placed the bowl beside them on the nightstand and removed his clothes, sitting up next to her on the headboard.

"If you're so interested in putting on a sexy show," she smiled at the three friends peering back at them from inside the bowl. "Don't let us stop you. Why don't you show us how you little people do it. You never know–maybe the king and I will pick up a few new tricks."

"Um..." Clover said, glancing nervously at her friends. "We hadn't planned on staying this long. If you let us go, we won't bother you or your daughter any longer."

"*Bother* us?" the queen smirked. "You're hardly bothering us. Quite the contrary. I find you quite alluring in your own little way. But if you're a bit bashful, I understand. I'll make you a deal. If you three put on an entertaining show for my husband and me, we'll let you go with no hard feelings."

"What exactly do you want us to do?" Clover said.

"Whatever you normally do," the queen said. "You must have some interesting moves in your repertoire to get my daughter so excited watching you. Just make love like you usually do and we'll follow your lead."

Clover peered at her two friends and they looked back at her, shaking their heads.

"Let's just give them what they want," Tara whispered. "If this is the only way out of here, they could have done much worse. All we have to do is put on a good show. Just fake it until they're satisfied, then hopefully they'll let us go."

Clover looked at Jessop and he shrugged his shoulders.

"I don't see any other way out of here," he said.

As the three friends pressed their bodies together, they started to kiss and grope one another. While they rocked their hips together awkwardly, the queen shifted in the bed beside them, lowering the covers to reveal her naked legs and pussy. She was actually quite attractive for a middle-aged woman, with firm, plump breasts and smooth, creamy skin. The thick bush between her legs glistened with a light dew as she began to roll her fingers over her wet vulva.

"Surely you can do better than that," she grumbled. "Let me see you touch your private parts. I want to see you make the boy hard."

Clover and Tara fanned out beside Jessop, stroking his cock and balls from both sides as he began to groan softly.

"*That's* more like it," the queen said, reaching over to caress her husband's dormant pecker. "You like a nice handjob once in a while too, don't you, dear?"

The king grunted as his wife squeezed his organ between her fingers, cupping his balls with her other hand. Within seconds, his penis began to expand and rise between his legs until it stood proudly erect, flapping and pulsing as she stroked it softly along its entire length. Although it was normally proportioned with the rest of his body, because of his enormous size, his erect cock towered six feet above his belly instead of the customary six inches. As Clover and Tara wrapped their hands around Jessop's hardening dick, they stared at the king's enormous tool with wide eyes.

"Your boy's fairly well-equipped for someone his size," the queen smiled, rolling her thumb over her husband's dripping glans. "I bet you've never seen a man's organ as big as this one before. Get down on your knees and suck that boy's cock while you finger your girlfriend's pussy. My husband's beginning to enjoy this little show."

As Clover knelt down in front of Jessop to take his penis into her mouth, Tara reached under her ass to circle her flaring nub.

"*Yes*," the queen panted, placing her other hand between her legs as she thrust two fingers into her slit while she stroked the king's giant cock as he watched the trio. "Is this turning you on, boy? Do you like watching me jerk the king's huge cock while your girlfriend sucks your dick? Let's see which of you can last longer. My husband's already starting to spill his seed watching your girlfriend's tight ass bouncing in front of your prick."

As Clover, Tara, and Jessop began rocking their hips more vigorously in rising pleasure, the queen kneeled over the king's pole with her body facing the bowl and lowered herself onto his flapping phallus. As she began bobbing up and down over his prick, her full breasts bounced on her chest while she reached down, squeezing his balls.

"Are you enjoying the show a little more now, sweetheart?" she said, pinching her nipples with her other hand.

"Nnn-huh," the king nodded, rocking his hips in tandem with his wife as he stared at the naked threesome fucking each other in the glass bowl. As they began breathing more heavily from the action of their combined movements, the inside of the bowl started to fog up, and the king swiped his hand along the outside edge, trying to clear his view.

"I think our friends are beginning to enjoy themselves in their little glass house," the queen smiled. "Are you getting close, dear? Do you want to come inside my pussy while you watch these pretty girls servicing their friend?"

"*Fuck* yes," the king said as he grasped the sides of the queen's ass and thrust his giant cock harder into her slurping pussy. When he finally came, he let out a bellow that echoed throughout the bed chamber, creating a ringing sound inside the hollow bowl. The strange vibration seemed to elevate the excitement of the connected threesome, and before long, each of them began shaking and moaning from their own climaxes.

After everybody recovered from their powerful orgasms, Clover looked up at the king and queen lying together on the bed.

"Can we go now?" she said. "We fulfilled our end of the bargain and you both seemed to enjoy the show."

"I didn't say exactly *when* I was going to let you go," the queen smiled. "We're just getting started. I have plenty of *other* ideas for how you can keep us amused."

4

————————

"What *else* can you possibly want us to do?" Clover said, still trying to catch her breath. "At least you can remove the cover to the bowl so we can breathe. There's hardly any air in here."

"I don't think you'll need to stay in that bowl much longer," the queen smiled. "I was thinking of some more *direct* involvement for your next step in the entertainment."

Clover peered up at the king's giant cock still resting against his belly, dripping rivulets of cum down over his huge balls.

"But we're far too small to stimulate you directly," she said. "Your body parts would never fit–"

"Not *all* of our body parts are large," the queen said, pinching her nipples as she peered at Clover's wet snatch. "And not all of *yours* are so tiny. Some of them are made to stretch a little, are they not?"

"Well yes, but nothing that could accommodate that enormous cock..."

"Who said anything about a *cock*?" the queen smiled,

removing the book from the top of the bowl and reaching in to lift Clover by her shoulders, placing atop her plump bosom. "There are plenty of other parts of that can be fun to play with. Lick my nipples while you rub your pretty ass over my tits."

Clover peered at the queen's nipples standing erect atop her huge breasts, and pinched her eyebrows. Looking more the size of a *soda can* than a regular teat, it was hard for her to imagine how she could get her mouth around them, let alone any other part of her body. She looked at her friends sliding down the inside of the fruit bowl as they tried to climb out, then peered back up at the queen.

"Will you let my friends go if I satisfy your wishes?"

"Soon enough, dear," the queen said, lifting Clover up and positioning her overtop one of her nipples. "Besides, this isn't exactly a negotiation."

Clover paused for a moment peering at the pink flesh of the queen's nipple, then she placed her hands around its perimeter, squeezing it like a giant sausage. It looked more like a fat *cock* this close-up, and as she began to stroke it, it began to swell and extend upward from the surface of the queen's trembling breast.

"Mmm," that feels good, she purred. "Give me a handie like I did for the king earlier. I've never felt anything quite like this before."

As Clover rolled her hands over the turgid stump, she sat atop the queen's breast, wrapping her legs over her areola to keep herself from slipping off.

"Yes, rub your wet pussy over my breast while you stroke my nipple," the queen moaned. "You have a sexy figure for a little person. I'd fuck you right proper if you were a little bigger."

As Clover's juices began to coat the skin around the queen's teat, she rubbed her hands into the lubrication, squeezing the nipple harder between her hands.

"Fuck yes," the queen hissed, grabbing hold of Clover's body and rubbing her slippery pussy harder against her tit. "Suck my teat while you stroke me with your hands. Pretend you're sucking your boyfriend's cock while you stroke his balls."

Clover widened her lips then lowered her mouth over the queen's nipple, flicking her tongue around the edges the way she knew Jessop liked it when she sucked his head. The feeling was not dissimilar, as she felt the erect nipple flexing and pulsing in her mouth.

"Oh *God* yes," the queen panted. "Just like that. I had no idea you little people could be so versatile. Wrap your legs around my nipple while you suck me. I want to feel your pussy rubbing my teat while you suck me."

Clover wrapped her legs tighter around the queen's tit and pressed her dripping vulva against the base of her nipple while she stroked and sucked it like a big penis. She was beginning to enjoy the unusual sensation, and as her juices began to dribble down over the queen's breast, the queen grasped Clover in her hand, placing her atop her tip.

"You seem to be enjoying this almost as much as I am," the queen smiled, forcing her down over her nipple. Clover felt the erect flesh press into her pussy, and she groaned feeling the bulge rub against her tingling clit.

"Yeah?" the queen sneered. "You like that? Do you like fucking my fat teats like your boyfriend's dick? It's just about the same size, isn't it?"

The queen peered over at Tara trying to scramble out of the bowl and picked her up with her other hand.

"No point wasting a perfectly good pussy when I've got *two* available teats," she said.

She placed Tara atop her other nipple in the same position as Clover, grasping the two girls firmly in her hands.

"This is what I call putting on a *truly* interactive show. Fuck my two nipples with your twats while the men imagine it's their dicks inserted into your pussies instead of my berries."

While the queen twisted and bounced the two girls' bodies atop her glistening breasts, Jessop and the king circled their hardening dicks with their fists as they watched the erotic show.

"Is this turning you boys on?" the queen mocked, spreading her legs apart to reveal her dripping pussy. "Do you want a piece of the real thing?"

"Don't mind if I do," the king said, rolling over to point his dick in front of the queen's pussy.

But she pushed him back down onto the bed, peering at Jessop jerking his pole as he watched his two friends fucking the queen's rigid tips.

"You've already *had* your turn," the queen smiled at her husband, reaching into the bowl to pick Jessop up.

She lifted him in front of her face then lapped her giant tongue over his bouncing hard-on.

"Do you like big girls once in a while?" she teased, flapping his hard-on from side to side with her thick appendage. "I bet you've never been deep-throated quite like *this* before."

The queen puckered her lips then pressed Jessop's cock deep into her mouth, lapping his balls with the base of her tongue as she rammed his body back and forth against her puffy lips. Jessop groaned in delight as his body slammed against her moist mouth, feeling the queen's breath blowing over him as she became increasingly turned on from the feeling of the two girls humping her teats.

"Fuck *this*," she said, rocking her hips impatiently.

She removed Jessop's tiny prick from her mouth and turned him upside down, positioning his feet in front of her dripping snatch.

"Let's try a *different* kind of full immersion this time," she smirked. "One we can *both* enjoy at the same time."

"But–" Jessop protested as he peered into the dark abyss of the queen's slit.

"Don't worry," she purred. "I won't hurt you. Just try to keep your legs stiff so I can imagine it's your dick inside me instead while I use you like a dildo. You might enjoy this as much as me."

As the queen inserted Jessop's rigid body into her hole, his look of apprehension soon turned to pleasure as her wet lubrication coated his entire body while she pulled him in and out of her hole. Within minutes, all four of the interconnected group were moaning in simultaneous delight, approaching the peak of their pleasure.

"Does that feel good, baby?" the queen said, noticing the look of ecstasy on Jessop's face as she pulled his bouncing hard-on in and out of her flapping lips.

"Yes," he groaned, staring at the queen's bulbous clit inches in front of his face.

"Get ready then, because I'm about to give you a different kind of shower when I come. Massage my clit while you fuck me with your legs."

Jessop jackknifed his body, then leaned forward, rolling the palms of his hands over the queen's slippery pearl while he felt her labia pressing harder against his sides. As she began to groan more loudly, suddenly he felt her pussy begin pulsing against his body as she began to squirt large jets of fluid out of her pussy, drenching his face and ass with her juices. Overwhelmed by the erotic scene playing out before him, he let go another giant-sized orgasm while the queen's cunt convulsed all around him.

W hen she finally stopped quivering from her three-way orgasm, the queen peered over at her husband who'd been stroking his cock watching all the excitement.

"What are we going to do about the king now?" she said, pulling Jessop out of her dripping hole. "We can't very well leave him to his own devices. He is the *king*, after all. He pays people to look after his personal needs. And he's looking pretty needy at this particular moment."

"What could we possibly do to help him?" Clover said, lifting herself off the queen's nipple as she and Tara peered at one another with flushed faces. "There's no way that thing would fit into any curve or crevasse of our bodies."

"Perhaps, not," the queen smiled. "But there's *three* of you and only *one* cock of his. I'm pretty sure you could find some creative ways to stimulate him if you put your minds to it."

She lifted the two girls up by their shoulders and placed them on either side of the king's rigid pole.

"Why don't you rub your pretty little tits against his stiffie and take it from there?"

"And then you'll let us go?" Clover said.

"Why are you in such a hurry to leave?" the queen said. "Haven't you been enjoying yourself so far?"

"Yes, but we're eager to get back home. Plus, our dragon will be wondering what happened to us."

"Dragons weren't meant to be friends with humans," the queen said. "I'm sure he'll fly off and find a new distraction soon enough. Unless you think he'd like to *join* us in the festivities. I imagine he must be getting pretty lonely and horny not being able to put his own oversize tool to better use."

"Ugh, no," Clover said, scrunching her face. "He's not like that with us. We'd never do anything like that with him."

"You never know if you might like it until you try," the queen said, nudging the girls' bodies with her finger. "Wrap your arms around my husband's organ and give him a new kind of handjob. I think he's become quite smitten with the two of you."

Clover peered at Tara and she frowned, indicating they didn't have much choice. They both knew that they were at the king and queen's mercy until they could find a way out of their predicament. In the meantime, they'd just have to do as they were told. As they wrapped their arms around the king's hard cock and began to bend their bodies up and down, he began to moan. Their heads were almost level with the tip of his tool, and as they pulled his foreskin forward and back, they could see the top of his dripping crown poking in and out of his sheath.

"Do you like that almost as much as when *I* give you a handjob?" the queen purred, cradling his balls.

"Fuck *yes*," the king said, wrapping his hand around the two girls while he squeezed them harder against his pulsing pole.

"Be careful you don't squeeze them too hard," the queen said. "We wouldn't want to crush them before they've finished servicing us. I can still think of a few ways they can be put to good use."

"So can *I*," the king said, pushing Clover's and Tara's faces against his sensitive glans. As precum began to pour out of his slit and down over their heads, they blinked their lids trying to keep the sticky fluid out of their eyes.

"I bet you've never been soaked in a man's cum quite like this before, have you girls?" the queen taunted, rubbing Jessop's slippery body over her still-tingling teats. "What about you, boy? Do you like cumming all over your girl-friends' faces?"

Jessop simply murmured as the queen swiped his body over her glistening tits, reveling in the feeling of her giant melons.

"Have you even been with a *man* before?" the queen said. "Sometimes it can be almost as much fun as being with a woman. Perhaps we can put you to better use while the girls are stroking my husband's cock."

She lowered Jessop between the king's legs, pressing his body against his balls.

"Why don't you see what you can do to add to my husband's pleasure? Then perhaps we can talk about letting you and your friends go."

Jessop peered up at Tara and Clover and they nodded for him to comply. With the king becoming get more and more aroused from their combined stimulation, it wasn't as if he was going to take no for an answer. Jessop peered at the giant testicles bobbing between the king's legs like a pair of cannon balls,and wrapped his arms around them, squeezing them gently. The king grunted, tilting his hips upward.

"It looks like the king approves of your technique," the queen nodded. "Maybe you can find something to do with your little prick while you're down there. There's another hole a little further down. What do you say, dear? Would you like a little *anal rimming* to add to your delight?"

"Umphf," the king grunted, spreading his legs further apart.

"I'll take that as a yes," the queen smiled. "Give it a go, boy. You never know what it feels like to fuck a man up the ass until you give it a try. I hear the anal sphincter is even tighter than a woman's pussy, even for a giant. I'd love to see my husband get fucked by a *man* for a change."

Jessop paused as he felt the king's cum dribbling down over his perineum toward the crack of his ass. As he rubbed his cock in the slippery fluid, he lowered his hips until he felt a wrinkled depression. As he pressed his hips forward, he felt his dick slip into the king's pucker, and they both groaned.

"Feels pretty *good*, right?" the queen smiled, looking at the picture of ecstasy on both of the men's faces. "They say the anus is surrounded with almost as many nerve endings as the penis and clitoris. Fuck my husband's ass hard while your girlfriends stroke his dick. It looks like he's getting ready to pop off any moment now."

As the king began to thrust his cock more rapidly between the girls' combined embrace, his pucker clenched tighter over Jessop's dick, and the two men began to groan approaching the peak of their pleasure. When the king came, he spurted a giant rope of cum high into the air, falling down over the heads of Jessop and the two girls, coating them in a thick layer of creamy syrup. While he grunted and continued spurting over the threesome, Jessop buried his cock in the king's sphincter, feeling his cock ejecting his own load inside the king's ass.

After what seemed like an eternity of showering the threesome in long strings of sticky cum, the king finally collapsed against the head of his bed as his wife ran her fingers over his dripping chest.

"There now," the queen purred, drawing slippery circles around his puffy nipples. "These little people aren't so bad after all, are they? Do you *still* want to flush them down the toilet?"

"Nuh-uh," the king shook his head, leaning over to kiss his wife passionately on her lips.

5

"So what happens now?" Clover said, trying to wipe the gobs of sticky cum off her body.

"I suppose we should get you cleaned up," the queen said. "That stuff will get hard and crusty before too long, then you'll hardly be able to move."

"And then will we be allowed to leave?"

"The only reason you're still alive is at the king's pleasure. Quite literally. As long as you continue to be of value to us, you'll be safe and well cared for."

"So you're going to hold us prisoner as your sex slaves?"

"It could be worse. You could have had a far more ignominious fate."

"Where are you going to keep us in the meantime?"

"That's a good question," the queen said, peering around her bed chamber. "Since you three seem hell-bent on leaving this place, we can't very well let you roam around freely, can we?"

She rested her gaze on a metal box resting in a corner of the room and got out of bed to retrieve it. Then she placed the three friends back in the bowl, filling it halfway with water. The metal box had some kind of trapdoor on the front, and she lifted it, placing the bowl inside. Then she lowered the gate and snapped a padlock over the corner to secure it shut.

"What's *this*?" Clover asked.

"Usually, it's a rat trap," the queen said. "But for the indefinite future, it's going to be your home."

"You're planning to lock us up in a fetid rat trap for the rest of our lives?" Tara screamed, stepping forward to shake the iron bars of the gate with her fists.

"It won't be so bad," the queen smiled, staring at Tara's sexy figure. "We'll have a maid come in periodically to clean it up and provide regular meals. In the meantime, you've got plenty of water and your own personal bath. We'll expect you to be properly cleaned up the next time the king and I want to resume our activities. I'm already thinking of how I'd like to put you to work during our next session."

"You'll never get away with this!" Tara railed, shaking the bars furiously.

"It hardly looks like you're in a position to be making threats," the queen said, stroking Tara's naked bush with the tip of her finger. "But I like your feisty attitude. That might come in handy at the right time. The king and I have some official duties to attend to now. If you need anything else, just let our maidservant know."

After the king and queen exited the bed chamber, the three friends leaned against the side of the cold metal box, staring at one another.

"Well, this is another fine mess you've gotten us into," Jessop sighed, peering at Clover.

"Perhaps you should have been thinking of a way out of it while you were fucking the king's bunghole," Clover said.

"It's not like I had much choice in the matter," he said. "I didn't exactly see you two looking for an escape route while you were rubbing your tits up against his fat cock."

"We've got to stop arguing if we're going to find a way out of here," Tara said. "It doesn't look like the king and queen have any plans to release us anytime soon."

"What the hell are we supposed to do locked up in a *rat cage*?" Jessop said, trying to budge the metal gate unsuccessfully. "That padlock is larger than the king's balls!"

"We still have a few resources at our disposal," Clover said, peering up at the giant lock secured to the top of the gate. "At least we seem to have made a friend of the king's *daughter*, and she seems disposed to helping us."

"That may be true," Jessop said. "But I'm sure the king has already considered that possibility and hidden the key in a place where she'll never find it."

"There's also the *maid*," Tara said. "Maybe we can explain our predicament to her and she can help us. If anyone could find the key, she'd presumably know where to look."

"And if not, what then?" Jessop said. "Spend the rest of our days as sex slaves to this giant ogre and his witch of a wife?"

"It was a little fun while it lasted," Tara nodded. "But I ran away from my clan to escape this kind of servitude. I don't plan to continue sucking up to these people, literally or figuratively."

"We've still got Rex," Clover said. "Maybe he could fly us out of here."

"That presumes he hasn't already flown off thinking we've abandoned him," Jessop said. "And even if he sticks around and somehow avoids capture himself, how are we going to sneak him into the king's bedroom?"

"And open this crate," Tara nodded. "He may be strong, but I'm not sure even *he* could bend these steel bars."

"Let's worry about that when the time comes," Clover said, peering up at the rim of the bowl a full body length above her. "With a little ingenuity, we should be able to figure a way out of this situation. In the meantime, I don't know about you guys, but I'm going to have a bath. Can somebody give me a hand getting back into the bowl? I don't plan on spending my idle time covered in the king's goop."

After the three friends had a long cleansing bath in the bowl, they climbed back out, falling asleep exhausted on the floor of the enclosure. A few hours later, they awoke to the sound of rustling bedsheets next to the box. They peered outside the front and saw a young girl dressed in a maid's outfit changing the king's bed linens.

"Hello!" Clover said, shaking the bars of the crate. "Can you hear me?"

The girl turned around and knelt down, peering into the box. She looked to be about Clover's age, in her late adolescence, with fair hair and bright green eyes. When she saw the three little naked people, her eyes widened and she gasped.

"Can you help us?" Clover said. "The king has locked us up in here and we just want to get back to where we came from."

"I'm sorry," the girl said, shaking her head. "But he gave

me express orders not do anything other than feed you and replace your water. I wish I could help, but he has a bad reputation for dealing with people who disobey his orders."

"I understand," Clover said. "Can you at least send word to his daughter Ophelia about our situation? Perhaps there's something *she* can do to help us."

"I'll try to send word to her when I have a free moment," the maid nodded. "In the meantime, I brought you some fresh food and provisions."

The girl slid some sliced carrots and celery through the bars and a flat piece of wood that looked like a cutting board.

"This will be something cleaner for you to sleep on than the dirty floor of the crate," she said, laying the board on the floor. Then she slipped a large cloth that looked like a giant hand towel through the narrow bars. "And this should provide a bit of warmth and cover for your naked bodies while you sleep."

"You're very kind," Clover said, passing the food around to her friends. "Have you got more drinking water too? We've got a full bowl behind us, but we've been bathing in it, and it's–well, not exactly *drinkable*."

"Of course," the girl said. "If you'll step back, I'll empty and refill it for you."

The three friends stepped toward the rear of the enclosure, and the girl tipped the bowl forward, holding a bucket under the front of the box as the water poured under the front of the gate. When the bowl had emptied, she wiped the inside of it with a cloth, then refilled it halfway with the long neck of a watering can. Before she left, she placed a small thimble inside the front of the enclosure, frowning toward Clover.

"I'm sorry to leave you with such crude provisions, but

for now at least this will provide a place for you to do your business. I'll come back twice a day to empty your privy and replace your provisions. Please let me know if there's anything else I can do for you."

As the girl stood to leave, Clover rushed forward, pressing her naked body against the front gate.

"Wait!" she said. "What's your name?"

"Penelope," the girl said.

"Thank you for taking care of us, Penelope," Clover said. "My name's Clover, and these are my friends Tara and Jessop. We might as well get to know one another since we might be here for a while."

"Nice to meet you, Clover," the girl said, pressing her finger through the bars to caress Clover's stomach. "I'm looking forward to getting to know all of you, as well."

When the girl turned to leave the bed chamber, Tara peered up at Clover, offering her a slice of celery.

"Well that went about as well as could be expected," she said. "At least we have some fresh food and water now."

"And hopefully a new ally," Clover nodded, watching the pretty girl exit the room.

"Yes," Jessop grinned. "I think our maid has a bit of a crush on Clover. Did you see the way she was looking at her naked body and how she was caressing her through the bars?"

"She's probably just curious about seeing little people this close-up," Clover said, blushing slightly.

"Maybe," Tara said. "But we might be able to work this little infatuation to our advantage. If the king and queen and their daughter seem so interested in using us for their carnal pleasure, maybe we can persuade the maid to find a way out of this rat trap by giving her a little erotic entertainment of her own."

"Possibly," Clover said, watching Jessop's flagging cock beginning to rise as he stared at the maid's tight ass while she left the room. "Or maybe she'll be more interested in *Jessop's* special skills the next time she returns to service the room."

6

A couple of hours later, the door to the king's bedroom creaked open and Penelope entered the room, followed by Ophelia close behind. Then they tiptoed up to the front of the three friends' crate and peered inside.

"Ophelia!" Clover said, rushing up to the entrance. "Thank heavens! Is there anything you can do to help us?"

Ophelia took a moment to inspect the metal cage trying to pull open the front gate, then shook the padlock that was securing it shut.

"This thing is built pretty solid," she said. "I don't think I'll be able to pry it open without some special tools."

"Have you got a crowbar or something?" Clover said. "All we need is a few extra inches between the bars and the side of the box to squeeze out."

"I should be able to find something," Ophelia nodded. "Has Penelope been taking good care of you?"

"Yes," Clover said, smiling up at the pretty maid. "She's helped make our situation bearable. But we've got to find a way out of here soon. I'm not sure what your mother and father plan to do with us. They've been talking about some pretty scary things."

"What about your dragon?" Ophelia said. "Maybe he can carry you to safety inside your crate."

"Is he still here?" Clover said, feeling her heart beginning to pound with renewed hope.

"Yes," Ophelia said. "I've been feeding him leftovers from my daily meals. I think he's grown quite fond of me."

"He seems to like anyone who gives him a regular lunch," Clover chuckled. "But I'm not sure he could lift this heavy crate very far. And even if he did, we'd still have the problem of getting it open. I don't think his lock-picking skills are quite as well advanced as his eating habits."

"I'll see what I can do about finding something to pry the gate open," Ophelia said, spreading her palms in front of the trio. "In the meantime, I brought your clothes so at least you can have something to cover up and keep you warm. I'm not sure your weapons will be much good in defending yourselves, but perhaps they can at least keep the family *cat* at bay if he gets too close to your box."

"Thank you," Clover said, passing the clothes back to her friends as they pulled them over their naked bodies.

Suddenly, they heard a scurrying sound outside the king's bedroom door, and the five friends peered at one another nervously.

"You better hide in case it's the king returning," Clover said. "There's no telling what he'll do to you two if he catches you helping us escape."

Ophelia and Penelope peered at one another with a frightened look, then scrambled under the king's bed just as the door swung open. The king and queen entered the room and closed the door behind them. Then the queen approached the crate sitting atop their nightstand and peered inside.

"I see the maid's managed to retrieve your clothing," she nodded. "But you won't be needing that soon enough. The king and I have been talking about some new ways we'd like to engage your services. The boy's cock was an interesting distraction, but he's far more interested in the girls' pretty little pussies."

"What could he possibly want with us?" Clover said. "There's no way he could ever fit inside our openings."

"Perhaps not with his *cock*," the queen smiled. "But there are *other* parts he can probe you with. His little finger isn't much bigger than the boy's erect penis. Then there's always his tongue. He has all kinds of plans for licking and molesting every part of your pretty bodies."

Tara suddenly stepped forward, pulling Jessop's sword out of its sheath, waving it threateningly in front of the bars.

"What makes you think we won't just *slice off* his finger or tongue if he gets too close to us?" she said.

"You're so cute with your little toy weapons," the queen chuckled. "I'm sure they come in handy catching the odd stray rabbit or fending off unwanted advances from other little people, but they're no match for our superior size and strength. Besides, if you don't cooperate with our commands, we can have you executed or worse. The king doesn't take kindly to anyone who doesn't follow his orders."

The queen smiled as she watched her husband remove his clothes, noticing his half-erect organ flapping against the side of his thigh.

"We're going to get cleaned up in the washroom then crawl back into bed to resume our little playtime. You'd be advised to do the same and remove your clothes in preparation for the next step in our merrymaking."

As soon as the king and queen retired to their powder room, Ophelia and Penelope rolled out from under the bed, and Ophelia lifted the crate off the nightstand.

"Where are you taking us?" Clover said, looking at her alarmed.

"I'm not sure yet, but we've got to get you out of here. From the sounds of it, my father intends to keep probing you until he tears you apart. Come, we'll figure out how to get you out of this box when we've got more time."

Ophelia and Penelope scurried out of the king's bedroom and closed the door quietly behind them, then they rushed down the hall toward the princess's bedroom, locking the door behind them. When they got inside, they hurried out onto the terrace where Rex flapped his wings excitedly when he saw his friends.

"Rex!" Clover said, rushing up to the front of the gate to pat the dragon's nose as he nuzzled up against the trio.

"So what do we do now?" Tara said with a worried expression. "It won't take long for the king and queen to find out that we've escaped, and this will be the first place he looks."

Ophelia peered around her room, looking for some kind of tool to pry open the entrance to the crate.

"The fireplace poker!" she said, rushing inside to retrieve the cast iron rod. "If that doesn't pry open the front cover, at least we should be able to puncture some holes in the metal large enough for you to crawl out."

When she returned with the poker, she wedged it between the side of the door and the edge of the box, straining to break it open. But the gate had a piece inserted into the base of the crate besides the side latch, and the bars only pulled apart far enough for the trio to squeeze their legs outside.

Suddenly they heard a loud pounding on Ophelia's door as the king bellowed from outside in the hall.

"Open this door immediately, Ophelia!" he yelled. "I know you have those little people in there, and you won't get away with it. If you don't open this door right away, I'll have my guards break it down!"

Ophelia and Penelope peered at one another with a frightened look, then Ophelia stepped back, raising the fireplace poker above her head.

"Step back toward the rear of the enclosure," she instructed the trio cowering inside. "I'm going to try bashing this thing open. Move to the corner where it won't hurt you."

The three friends looked at one another with wide eyes, then scrambled to the back corner behind the glass bowl. As Ophelia began hammering the top of the box with the fireplace poker, it shook violently and the water began shifting from side to side in the bowl, drenching their quivering bodies. While she continued bashing the crate, Rex screamed and flapped his wings around her head, worried that she was trying to harm them.

Suddenly there was a loud banging sound on the bedroom door, and the two girls peered through the terrace window, watching it beginning to shake and loosen on its hinges. Within seconds, the king and queen burst through the door followed by a contingent of guards. When they saw Ophelia and Penelope standing outside on the terrace holding the crate, they turned toward them with a scowl on their faces.

"Hand that over girls, and no one will get hurt," he said. "I know you're just trying to help your friends, but they belong to *us* now. This is no concern of yours any longer."

As the king and his guards approached the two girls, Ophelia peered at the three little people cowering inside the crate, then back at Rex who was still flapping his wings in the air, hissing toward the king's coterie.

"Here," she said, holding the crate up for Rex to grasp onto. "Fly your friends away to safety. If you can't manage to get out, come back when things quiet down and we'll find another way to get this thing open. But right now, you've got to get out of here!"

Rex grasped the side of the crate with his claws and began flapping his wings trying to lift it into the air, but the box was too heavy and he bobbed up and down as his nails began to slide over the slippery surface. Just as the king reached out to grab the crate, the dragon angled over the edge of the terrace, soaring downward, looking for a place to land. Clover and her friends could hear the sound of his claws slipping against the hard metal, and they peered around frantically, looking for somewhere to land.

"There!" she said, pointing to another terrace a few stories below. "Land there, boy, where you can get a better grip on the box. It will take a few minutes for the king to reach us down there. Maybe he can insert his claws into the holes Ophelia made to gain better traction."

Rex turned in the direction Clover was pointing, and as he glided down onto the platform, the box fell onto the tiled surface while he was about to land. The glass bowl shattered into a hundred pieces and the water poured over the trio, causing them to lose their footing and bounce up against the sides of the enclosure. Miraculously, nobody was seriously hurt, and as Rex ambled up to the front of the enclosure to peer inside, Clover tiptoed around the broken glass and reached outside the bars to stroke his head.

"Good boy, Rex," she said. "You did good. Do you think you can find a better way to grab hold of this box? Maybe wrap your claws around the front bars or the little holes in the top."

Rex titled his head at his friends, confused by what they were trying to say to him while he prodded the gate with his hind legs. As the crate tipped and turned with the trio bouncing around inside, Jessop yelped when a sharp shard of glass punctured his leg.

"There's got to be another way out of this," Tara said, staggering up beside Clover as she motioned for Rex to stop batting the cage. "If Rex doesn't kill us by dropping us hundreds of feet onto the ground, the sharp glass will cut us to shreds."

"We better think of something quick," Jessop said, wrapping a piece of cloth around his leg. "I can already hear the king's guards rushing down to our level to capture us."

Clover peered up around the perimeter of the enclosure, searching for another solution. But the heavy steel crate hardly looked any worse for the wear, and she shook her head.

"This thing isn't built like the mousetraps where *I* come from," she said. "They really built this to resist any gnawing or clawing of any creatures trapped inside. As long as that giant padlock is holding the gate closed, I don't see another way out of here."

Tara squinted her eyes at the swinging lock at the top of the gate, then rushed forward, motioning to Rex.

"What if Rex could *burn* it off?" she said. "His breath can easily be turned into a blowtorch. If he breathes on it long enough, maybe he can melt it or at least break the seal."

"It's worth a try," Clover said, listening to the stomping sound of the guards' feet getting closer and closer to their platform.

"Blow your fire on the *lock*, Rex!" she said, pointing up to the latch and puffing her lips to simulate heavy breathing.

But he just peered at her curiously, wondering why she was acting so strange.

"*Great*," Jessop said. "We forgot to teach him *English* while we were learning to ride him. He has no clue what we're talking about."

Tara suddenly jumped on the front gate and began climbing up the bars to the top of the crate, shaking the padlock with her hands and feet.

"The *lock*, Rex!" she screamed, blowing on it with all her might. "Blow your fire on the *lock*, boy!"

Rex peered at Tara with a puzzled expression then he nodded his head, seeming to understand what she was saying. He tapped the front of the gate softly with his claw, and Tara climbed down, moving to the back of the crate with the others to escape the flame. When they were as far from the front of the cage as possible, Rex reared back and opened his mouth, sending a searing fireball toward the padlock. The temperature in the enclosure quickly rose from the blowback of his breath, and the trio pulled their feet back, watching the pool of water on the floor of their enclosure begin to steam and boil.

Clover noticed the padlock swinging from the force of the dragon's breath, and as it slowly began to melt, she gripped her friends' hands tightly.

"Let's hope he gets that thing off before he *fries* us all to death," Jessop said, holding the girls with all his might.

After a minute or two, the remains of the lock fell from the top of the crate onto the floor of the terrace and the trio rushed forward, trying to shake the front gate loose. But it still seemed to be locked tightly as they it rattled in their hands.

"Shit!" Jessop said, shaking the bars furiously. "It seems just as tight as ever. I hope Rex didn't fuse the bars to the side of the crate when he burned off the lock."

"Rex," Clover said, motioning for the dragon to come closer to the front of the crate while she shook the bars together with her friends. "Can you pull this off with your claws? It should be loose enough to pry off now."

Rex turned his head from side to side watching his friends trying to loosen the gate, then he curled the claws of one foot between the bars while he pressed his other foot against the front of the enclosure. As he grunted trying to pull the door off, the three friends heard the door to the adjoining room suddenly burst open.

"You can do it, buddy!" she said, urging the dragon on. "Pull with all your strength! We haven't got much time."

Rex groaned as he shook the crate with all his strength while the three friends held onto the bars to keep from falling onto the shifting shards of broken glass and hot water on the floor. As the king and his guards stormed onto the terrace, the gate suddenly burst open and the three friends tumbled out onto the tiled floor.

"There they are!" the king shouted, pointing to the dragon still grasping the grate with the trio clinging on.

The guards rushed forward, and Rex took flight, dangling the gate beneath him with the three friends holding on for dear life. As he flapped his wings soaring over the edge of the balcony, a shower of arrows flew past them while they listened to the king's screaming receding into the distance.

7

Ten minutes later, Rex glided to a clearing in the surrounding forest, and the three friends tumbled off the twisted grate, exhausted and shivering in fright.

"Holy crap!" Jessop said. "That was insane! Talk about a close call. We almost didn't make it out of there."

"We were pretty lucky," Clover nodded. "We could have died a hundred different ways. If the king didn't get us, we could just as easily have been burned alive inside the metal crate or fallen to our deaths when Rex whisked us away."

"I think I've had enough excitement for a little while," Tara sighed, touching the bruises on her body gingerly.

"Is everyone alright?" Clover said, looking at Jessop's bleeding leg. "How deep is that cut, Jessop?"

Jessop pulled the bandage off his leg and winced looking at the three-inch-wide gash.

"It doesn't look too bad," he said, touching it tenderly.

"What do you think, Tara?" Closer said, turning to her friend. "Can you patch him up?"

"It's not too deep," she nodded. "Another couple of

inches to the left and it would have sliced his femoral artery. But I can stitch it up pretty easily. It shouldn't take more than a week or two to heal up."

"Good," Clover said, patting Rex gently on his head as the dragon peered at the disheveled trio with a concerned look. "You did great, boy. Thanks for waiting around for us."

"So, what now?" Tara said. "Shouldn't we clear out of here before the king sends a search party out looking for us?"

"We'll be pretty hard to find in this dense cover," Clover said, peering around her. "I don't know about you guys, but I could use some hot food for a change. I'm tired of munching on carrots and celery. Why don't we try to scare up some rabbits and a boar for Rex? He's certainly earned it."

After Tara stitched up Jessop's wound, the three friends went foraging for food then built a campfire where they roasted three rabbits and a wild pig over a spit. After they checked the perimeter to make sure nobody was looking for them, they curled up under Rex's wings and fell fast asleep, resting until after dawn. When they woke up, they finished the rest of their food scraps, kneeling in a circle to discuss their next steps.

"Where should we go now?" Jessop said, peering at the two girls.

"As far away from here as possible," Tara said.

Clover paused as she contemplated their next move.

"What?" Tara said, looking at her suspiciously. "You don't agree? After the king wanted to poke and prod us with his greasy fingers and God knows what else? Haven't you had enough of this place? They weren't much help finding your precious waterfall. We might as well continue heading south and see what we can find. There's nothing else keeping us here."

"Maybe not," Clover said. "It's just–"

"What *other* possible reason could you have for sticking around here?" Jessop said. "Don't tell me you've developed *feelings* for the princess and her pretty maid?"

"We never got to thank them and give them a proper goodbye," Clover said. "The least we can do is express our gratitude for saving our lives."

"Are you *crazy*?" Tara said, widening her eyes. "You want to go back there?"

"Just for a few minutes. The king and queen will never be expecting us. We can stop just long enough on the terrace to say goodbye. As long as we don't go inside, we should be able to make a hasty exit if need be."

Tara and Jessop looked at one another, shaking their heads.

"You said you were looking for adventure when you ran away from the Norseland," Tara said. "Stick around and you never know what kind of surprises you might run into."

"You guys are crazy, you know that, right?" Jessop said.

"Yeah, but I bet you never imagined having a wild orgy with a bunch of giants," Clover smiled.

"Or screwing one up the ass," Jessop chuckled.

"Was it as much fun as doing it with a *girl*?" Tara said.

"When you're balls-deep in someone's else's hole, you don't pay much attention to who you're fucking. Although I'd far rather bury my face in your pretty tits than the king's hairy balls."

"It's settled then," Clover said, rising to put out the camp-fire and collect their things. "Maybe you'll get lucky and catch a glimpse of a few more pretty tits when we fly back to the castle. I have a feeling Ophelia will be practicing some of the new techniques we showed her on our first day up there."

The three friends climbed on Rex's back and Clover pulled back on his ears, steering him back in the direction of the castle. When they flew past the princess's bedroom, she squinted through the terrace windows, noticing some movement on her bed. As they glided closer, her eyes flew open when they saw Ophelia and Penelope writhing naked on the bed with their hips locked in a tight scissor position. The group landed softly on the deck then crept slowly up to the glass.

"It looks like she didn't waste much time putting some of our lessons to work," Tara smiled, peering at the pretty couple grunting and groaning as they ground their pussies together.

"And Penelope too," Clover nodded. "It seems these two have become partners-in-crime in more ways than one."

"The king must have grounded his daughter for life after she helped us escape," Jessop said. "I'm just glad he didn't have Penelope beheaded for her role in the escapade."

"They definitely seem to have found a confidant in one another," Clover said, beginning to feel her *own* loins moistening as she watched the two girls groaning and sighing.

"I think we better leave them alone now," Tara said, nudging Clover with the side of her hips. "I'm pretty sure they wouldn't want to be interrupted at this particular moment."

"I suppose not," Clover said, feeling some heavy breathing coming over her shoulder.

She turned around and saw Rex poking his face forward, peering at the two moaning girls with wide eyes. She glanced between his legs and noticed his giant cock slowly pressing out of its sheath.

"Apparently we awakened more than the *girls'* interest in

some extra-curricular activity," she smiled. "It looks like *Rex* is in need of a little companionship of his own."

Tara turned around and gasped when she saw the dragon's enormous pecker flexing between his legs.

"Well, we *do* have some experience massaging something that big," she smiled. "Maybe we should give him a little handie like we gave the king."

"What?" Clover said, scrunching up her face. "No, we should find a proper mate for him to play with."

"Where the hell are we going to find another dragon?" Jessop said.

"I'm not sure," Clover said, climbing on Rex's back. "But that sounds as good a new venture as any. Let's go see what we can find."

R eady for more erotic chills and thrills? Order the next exciting volume in Clover's Fantasy Adventures:

*Humans and elves aren't the only ones with sexual appetites
in the land of Abbynthia...*

ALSO BY VICTORIA RUSH

Wet your whistle a hundred different ways with Jade's Erotic Adventures. Browse the full collection of Victoria Rush steamy stories here:

Click to scan your favorites...

FOLLOW VICTORIA RUSH:

Want to keep informed of my latest erotic book releases? Sign up for my newsletter and receive a FREE bonus book:

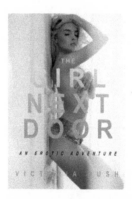

Spying on the neighbors just got a lot more interesting...

Printed in the USA
CPSIA information can be obtained
at www.ICGtesting.com
LVHW091606210424
778012LV00009B/519